When I grew up in England, a long time ago, I remember jumping rope to this rhyme. Although it was great fun, I was always puzzled by the fact that we never knew if Miss Polly's dolly recovered from her illness, because the rhyme finished when the doctor prescribed the pill for her. Did the doctor's pill do the trick? No one could answer my question because there wasn't a second verse. I came to live in America and found that American children jumped rope to the same rhyme. I began to wonder if any of these children were like me and wanted to know what happened to Dolly. So, I decided I would finish off the story myself and put everyone's mind at rest. Now I feel much happier knowing that Dolly was a good girl, took the pill given to her by the clever doctor and recovered quickly because she was so well looked after by Miss Polly. I hope you all look after your dollies and make sure that they are wrapped up so that they don't catch cold in the winter.

—P.D.E.

Miss Polly Has a Dolly

Retold by PAMELA DUNCAN EDWARDS

Illustrated by ELICIA CASTALDI

G. P. Putnam's Sons • New York

For Jum and Sam Symons and their grandchildren—P.D.E.

To Mom, Dad, and Joseph—E.C.

Manufactured in China by South China Printing Co. Ltd. Designed by Marikka Tamura. Text set in Maiandra Demi.
The art was done using painting and collage techniques, with finishing touches done on the computer.
Library of Congress Cataloging-in-Publication Data
Edwards, Pamela Duncan. Miss Polly has a dolly / retold by Pamela Duncan Edwards; illustrated by Elicia Castaldi.   p. cm.
Summary: Rhyming tale of a sick dolly, the care she receives from her doctor and Miss Polly,
and the treat she is offered when she becomes well.
[1. Dolls—Fiction. 2. Medical care—Fiction. 3. Stories in rhyme.] I. Castaldi, Elicia, ill. II. Title.
PZ8.3.E283 Mi 2003   [E]—dc21   2002153865
ISBN 0-399-23857-3
1 3 5 7 9 10 8 6 4 2
First Impression

Miss Polly has a dolly who is sick, sick, sick

She calls for the doctor to come quick, quick,

The doctor comes with his bag and his hat

And he knocks on the door

with a rat-a-tat-tat.

He looks at the dolly
and he shakes his head

He says, "Miss Polly, put her straight to bed."

He writes on his pad for a pill, pill, pill

Miss Polly has a dolly

good as gold, gold, gold

She's sure to take the pill when she is told, told, told.

"Dolly," says Miss Polly, "It is probably best

If I tuck you up for a nice long rest."

Miss Polly's little dolly goes right to sleep

The doctor pops in and he takes a peep.

That you've looked after Dolly

very well, well, well."

Miss Polly has a dolly who's now fit, fit, fit

She doesn't feel sick, not one bit, bit, bit!

"Miss Polly," says the doctor with a great big beam,

"Let's take the dolly out for . . .

"ice cream,

Miss Polly Has a Dolly

Retold by Pamela Duncan Edwards
Musical arrangement by Christopher Drobny
Copyright © 2003

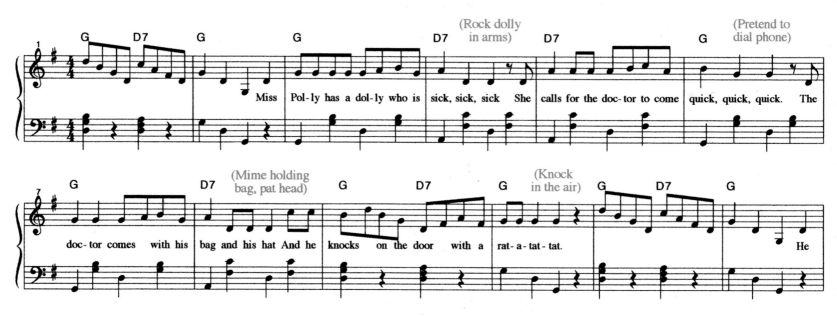